Copyright © 1986 Laurie Lattig-Ehlers
Published by PICTURE BOOK STUDIO,
an imprint of Neugebauer Press, Salzburg-Munich-London-Boston.
Distributed in USA by Alphabet Press, Natick, MA.
Distributed in Canada by Vanwell Publishing, St. Catharines.
Distributed in UK by Ragged Bears, Andover.
Distributed in Australia by Hodder & Stoughton Australia Pty, Ltd..
All rights reserved.
Printed in Austria.

LIBRARY OF CONGRESS CATALOGING IN PUBLICATION DATA

Lattig-Ehlers, Laurie.
Canoeing.

Summary: Describes the sights and sounds of a quiet canoe journey
down the river at dusk when the herons, owls, bats, and deer come out.
[1. Canoes and canoeing—Fiction. 2. River—Fiction. 3. Night—Fiction.
4. Animals—Fiction]
I. Gantschev, Ivan, ill. II. Title.
PZ7.L36995Can 1986   [E]   86-8180
ISBN 0-88708-029-4

Ask your bookseller for these other PICTURE BOOK STUDIO books
illustrated by Ivan Gantschev:
TWO ISLANDS
THE JOURNEY OF THE STORKS
THE VOLCANO
RUMPRUMP
THE MOON LAKE
NOAH & THE ARK & THE ANIMALS by Andrew Elborn
SANTA'S FAVORITE STORY by Hisako Aoki

Laurie Lattig-Ehlers

CANOEING

illustrated by Ivan Gantschev

PICTURE BOOK STUDIO

It is a summer evening, warm and sweet,
we are going canoeing.
We climb down to the river
holding the boat over our heads.
The low sun shines hot on our backs,
but the water's coolness drifts up to meet us.
Leaning together, we drop the canoe into the river.
It tips up then back and settles quietly.
We tie our shoes onto the bars and step in.
Pausing a moment in excitement, we push off.

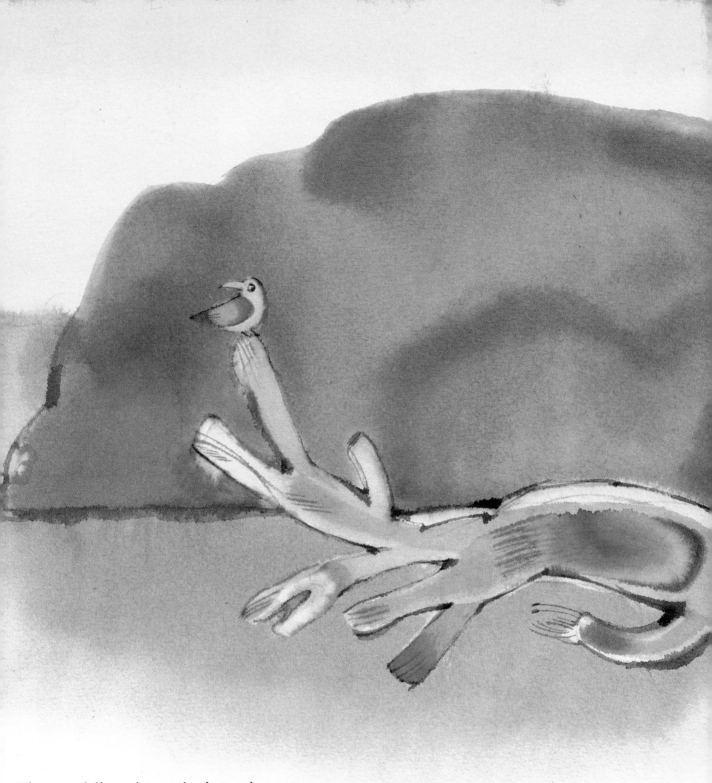

The paddles dip-splash in the water
and we pull away.
There are people on a distant shore laughing around a fire.
We float by, leaving them behind.
The canoe barely licks the water as we stop paddling.
It is so still.

Fir trees, wild grasses, horsetails;
 the shoreline follows as the current takes us
  down, down the river.
 Suddenly we hear a strange cry.

The blue grouse are dancing!
 They fan their tails out and back
  weaving around on the sand.
 White and black flash in the last bit of sun.

They call again
      but their cries are lost
   to the river's soft roar...

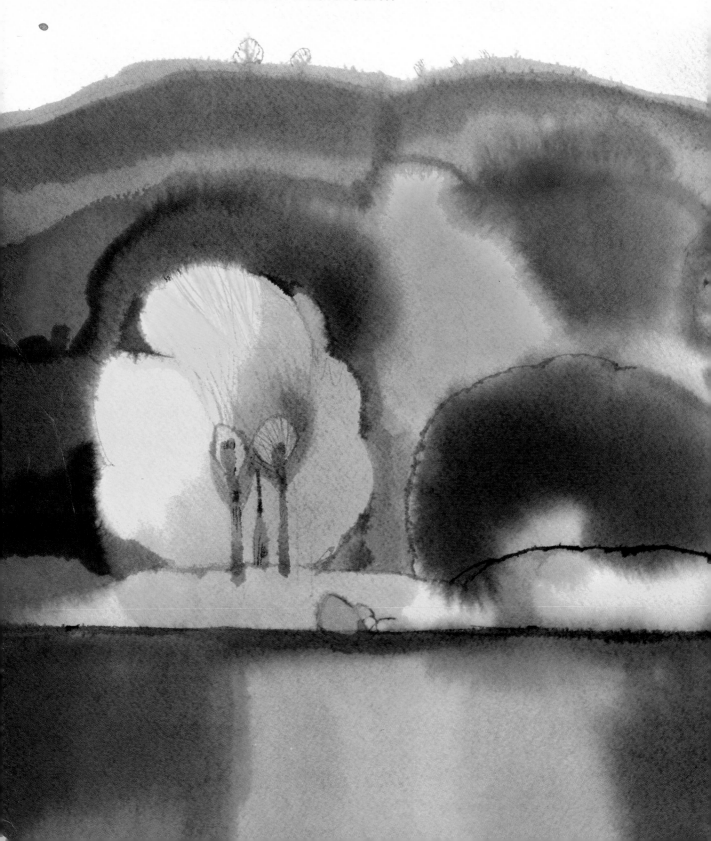

...Rapids are coming!
White water foams around the bow of the canoe,
cold spray covers us.
It's a wild, shivery ride
but we are sorry
as soon as it's over.

Calm again.
The sky is lines of peach and blue.
Fingers of violet outline spaces
soon to be filled by shadows of night.

A doe, soft in brown, draws near the water
guarded by the gentle light.
She trembles in river grasses, watching.
Before we pass, she slips into the shadows.

Swooping down from dark places,
the bats are out!
Flick-flick!
As close as they dare in lightning flutters.
We are caught in their night
frightening the peaceful waters.

Silver flashes in the first star light.
Water beetles swim fast
to hide under leaves,
while the river fish jump for their supper.

Hungry bullfrog voices sound from the land.
Invisible complainers, quiet now as we go by.

Tiny hands splash through the stillness.
Washing, the raccoons stop
    to wonder at us over the water.
Noses twitch in black fur faces
    until the canoe leaves their shoreline.
We paddle on.
    The river shimmers —
    dark mirror in the moonlight.

White wings slip over the water,
       they ruffle near a tall pine and disappear.
Nothing moves on the land.
          The great owl is keeping his watch,
             friend only to the night.
              Whoo… echoes whooo… across the river.
             The fish are still
                under circles of water.

A heron wings silently overhead
only a crooked neck against the moon.
Her mate calls from the shore.
She glides carefully around us
into darkness.
Far off lights flicker
reaching through the night
to call us back to shore.

Slipping between the rocks into the cove,
　　the canoe nestles against the sand.
For a moment we rest there,
　　hushed by gentle waters.
　　Slowly we lift the canoe out of the water,
　　up, and over our heads.
It is dark now.
We are going home.